BOOM CHICKA BOOM

✻ Stories, rhymes and funny verse ✻ old and new ✻

Liz Weir is a storyteller, and makes her living
performing to live audiences.

ALSO AVAILABLE ON TAPE AND CD

D1200253

Liz Weir

After a distinguished career as a children's librarian,
Liz took the brave step into the world of performance.
Based in County Antrim, she now makes her living as
a storyteller, travelling to many countries, as well as
all over Ireland and Britain, telling stories to adults and
children. She has also worked on radio, presenting and
scripting the BBC's 'Gift of the Gab' programmes.

Thanks are due to many storytellers
who have swapped and shared these and other stories over
the years. These include: Bob Gasch (Minnesota),
Patrick Ryan (London via Illinois), Billy Teare (Ireland),
Carolyn Sue Thomas (Nebraska),
Cathryn Wellner (Canada), Duncan Williamson (Scotland),
and the children of Belfast who gave me
the rhyme 'Boom-Chicka-Boom'.

BOOM CHICKA BOOM

* A Book of Stories and Rhymes to Share *

Liz Weir

Illustrated by Josip Lizatovic

THE O'BRIEN PRESS
DUBLIN

First published 1995 by The O'Brien Press Ltd.,
20 Victoria Road, Rathgar, Dublin 6, Ireland.

Copyright text © Liz Weir
Copyright © design, illustrations, recording: The O'Brien Press Ltd.

All rights reserved. No part of this book may be reproduced or utilised,
in any form or by any means, electronic or mechanical, including photocopying,
recording, or by any information storage and retrieval system without permission in
writing from the publisher. This book may not be sold as a bargain book or at a
reduced price without permission in writing from the publisher.

1   2   3   4   5   6   7   8   9   10
9 5   9 6   9 7   9 8   9 9   0 0   0 1   0 2

British Library Cataloguing-in-publication Data
Weir, Liz
Boom-chicka-boom – (Storytelling Series)
I. Title II. Lizatovic, Josip
III. Series
823 [J]

ISBN 0-86278-417-4

The O'Brien Press receives assistance from
The Arts Council / An Chomhairle Ealaíon.

Typesetting, editing, layout: The O'Brien Press Ltd.
Cover photographs: Amelia Stein
Cover design: The O'Brien Press
Cover separations: Lithoset Ltd., Dublin
Printing: The Guernsey Press Company Ltd.
Recording: Pine Valley Studios, Dublin
Producer: Liz Sweeney
Music: Joe Ó Dubhghaill

DEDICATION

*For my mother Nell Martin
and, of course, for Clare*

Contents

SIDE 1

Going to Granny's 9 (4.37min.)

Master of All Masters 16 (5.31min.)

Boom-Chicka-Boom 28 (1.31min.)

Long Bony Finger 30 (3.36 min.)

Rathlin Fairy Tale 37 (5.40 min)

TOTAL TIME 21.05 min.

SIDE 2

The Rabbit's Tale 45 (5.32 min.)

Wee Meg Barnileg 53 (7.41min.)

A Riddle Story 66 (1.23 min.)

The Tailor and the Button 70 (3.52 min.)

TOTAL TIME 18.38 min.

Going to Granny's

A participation story for everyone to join in with –
help pack Susie's case, get settled in for the night,
and choose her companions.

Susie was going to stay with her
Granny for the holidays. She packed
her bag, putting in her socks, shoes, vest,
pants, jeans, t-shirts, pyjamas and lots of
other clothes, until it was full to the very
top. She took a book to read, a special toy
to play with and a big bunch of bright
yellow flowers for Granny.

When she got to Granny's, she ran into
the bedroom (*beat hands on knees*), she

hopped into bed (*clap hands*), Granny
pulled up the covers (*hands drawing up
covers*), gave her a big kiss (*smack lips*),
flicked off the light (*click fingers*), closed
the squeeea-ky door (*make a nice squeaky
noise!*) – and Susie went: 'Eeh! Eeh! Eeh!'

Granny said: 'What's wrong, Susie?'

And Susie said: 'I'm lonely in here all by
myself! I need something to keep me
company.'

'Well,' said Granny, 'tomorrow night you can take the puppy to bed with you.'

So, the next night Susie ran into the bedroom, she hopped into bed, the puppy hopped into bed, Granny pulled up the covers, gave her a big kiss, flicked off the light, closed the squeaky door . . .

'Eeh! Eeh! Eeh!'

'Wuf! Wuf! Wuf!'

Granny said: 'What's wrong now, Susie?'

And Susie said: 'I'm still lonely.'

'Well,' said Granny, 'tomorrow night you can take the kitten to bed with you.'

So, the next night Susie ran into the
bedroom, she hopped into bed, the puppy
hopped into bed, the kitten hopped into
bed, Granny pulled up the covers, gave
her a big kiss, flicked off the light, closed
the squeaky door . . .

'Eeh! Eeh! Eeh!'

'Wuf! Wuf! Wuf!'

'Miaow! Miaow! Miaow!'

Granny said: 'What's wrong *now*, Susie?'

And Susie said: 'I'm still lonely.'

'Well,' said Granny, 'tomorrow night
you can take the lamb to bed with you.'

So, the next night Susie ran into the bedroom, she hopped into bed, the puppy hopped into bed, the kitten hopped into bed, the lamb hopped into bed, Granny pulled up the covers, gave her a big kiss, flicked off the light, closed the squeaky door . . .

'Eeh! Eeh! Eeh!'

'Wuf! Wuf! Wuf!'

'Miaow! Miaow! Miaow!'

'Baa! Baa! Baa!'

Granny said: '*What's wrong now*, Susie?'

And Susie said: 'I'm still lonely.'

'Susie,' said Granny, 'tomorrow night is your last night and I have only one animal left! I suppose you can take the horse with you tomorrow night.'

So, the next night Susie ran into the bedroom, she hopped into bed, the puppy hopped into bed, the kitten hopped into bed, the lamb hopped into bed – and the horse hopped into bed!

The bed went CRASH! and the floor went CRASH! and Granny's whole house went CRRRAAASH!

Poor Granny had to go out and buy a new house – but this time she was clever. She bought a house with a big strong floor and a big strong bed that was big enough and strong enough to hold a little girl called Susie and a puppy and a kitten and a lamb and most of all – a HORSE!

Master of All Masters

*A traditional English folk tale with opportunities
for children to join in the repetition
– and test their memories!*

Years ago, there used to be hiring fairs all over the country. Farmers would come looking for workers to plough, to milk the cattle and keep house. Young men and women would go to these fairs looking for work. They could often stand all day long waiting for a farmer to come and pick them out.

Now, there was a young girl called Jinny who had always been small and delicate,

and because of this no-one seemed to want to hire her. She stood shivering with cold long after her brothers and sisters had gone off to their new jobs. Now, Jinny was a clever girl, but how was anyone to know that just by looking at her?

Finally, at the end of the day as she was giving up hope of finding a place, a funny-looking old man came along, peered at her and said: 'Come along there, girl, don't dawdle!'

Jinny picked up her bundle, bid her parents farewell and set off after her new master.

'Now, girl, if you want to keep this job you must follow my instructions – exactly as I say.'

'Yes, sir,' said Jinny.

'We'll start there. What should you call me?'

'Why, master or mister, or whatever you please, sir.'

'NO! NO! NO! My name is *Don Nippery Septo, Master of All Masters*, and DON'T YOU FORGET IT!'

They soon came to a long, low, thatched cottage .

'Now, what would you call that?' he asked.

'Why, it's a house, or cottage, or whatever you please, sir.'

'NO! NO! NO! That's the *great castle of straw bungle*, and DON'T YOU FORGET IT!'

Into the house they went and there was a lovely roaring fire in the hearth.

'What's that?'

'Why, it's a fire, or a flame, or whatever you please, sir.'

'NO! NO! NO! That's the *hot cockalorum*, and DON'T YOU FORGET IT!'

Poor Jinny was beginning to panic, there was so much to learn.

Beside the fire a big black-and-white cat sat licking her paws.

'What would you call that?'

'Why, it's a cat or kitten, or whatever you please, sir.'

'NO! NO! NO! That's the *white-faced simony,* and DON'T YOU FORGET IT!'

On the other side of the hearth was a bucket of water – surely that was simple enough.

'What's that?'

'Why, it's water or wet, or whatever you please, sir.'

'NO! NO! NO! That's the *pondolorum*, and DON'T YOU FORGET IT!'

How many more new things would there be to learn, thought poor Jinny?

The old man pointed into the corner at a settle bed and he said: 'That's your place.

What would you call that?'

'Why, it's a bed or cot, or whatever you please, sir.'

'NO! NO! NO! That's your *barnacle*, and DON'T YOU FORGET IT!'

'Now, here's some washing – what would you call these?'

He held up a pair of trousers and Jinny said: 'Why, trousers or breeches, or whatever you please, sir.'

'NO! NO! NO! Those are my *squibs and crackers,* and DON'T YOU FORGET IT!'

He held up each boot in turn for the young girl to pull off. 'And what are these?'

'Why, boots or shoes, or whatever you please, sir.'

'NO! NO! NO! Those are my *hey down treaders*, and DON'T YOU FORGET IT!'

Pointing to a flight of steps he gave her a final piece of advice.

'Now, I'll be asleep up there. Remember all I've taught you and you'll keep your job. What would you call these?' With the final question he pointed at the stairs themselves.

'Why, steps or stairs, or whatever you please, sir.'

'NO! NO! NO! That's the *wooden hill*, and DON'T YOU FORGET IT!'

His words rang in Jinny's ears long after he had climbed up into the loft.

How was she ever going to remember all those new words? She tossed and turned, not getting a wink of sleep for trying to keep them all in her head.

Now, it was a good thing that Jinny was such a bright girl, for in the middle of the night she heard a terrible YOWL. What was going on?

Jinny leapt out of bed, saw what had happened, and then ran up the stairs roaring at the top of her voice:

'*Don Nippery Septo, Master of All Masters!* Quick! Quick! Get out of your *barnacle*, pull on your *squibs and crackers* and your *hey down treaders*, run down the *wooden hill*, for the *white-faced simony* has put her tail in the *hot cockalorum* and unless you get some *pondolorum* to put out the *hot cockalorum* the whole great *castle of straw bungle* will be on *hot cockalorum!*'

Boom-Chicka-Boom

(An echo chant! Just repeat the lines.)

VOICE:	I said a-boom-chicka-boom
RESPONSE:	I said a-boom-chicka-boom
VOICE:	I said a-boom-chicka-boom
RESPONSE:	I said a-boom-chicka-boom
VOICE:	I said a-boom-chicka-rocka-chicka-rocka-chicka-boom
RESPONSE:	I said a-boom-chicka-rocka-chicka-rocka-chicka-boom
VOICE:	All right?
RESPONSE:	All right?
VOICE:	Uh huh!
RESPONSE:	Uh huh!
VOICE:	One more time
RESPONSE:	One more time

VOICE: Very fast ...

RESPONSE   Very fast ...

Repeat this chant several times, changing the style
according to the instruction given in the last line.

Suggested ways include:

VERY FAST, VERY POSH,
VERY CHEEKY, VERY QUIETLY.

Try to think up some more – maybe very happy,
very jolly, very weepy ... !

On the final verse end like this:

All right?

All right?

Uh huh!

Uh huh !

No more times!

Long Bony Finger

*A scary story with an element of surprise
in which Sam gets his come-uppance.*

Now, Sam was a boy who loved to read ghost stories. Whenever he went to the library he was always sure to pick scary books. And he was always playing tricks on his friends to scare them as well.

One day Sam's friend Peter asked him over to his house after school. His Mum and Dad said he could go – but they warned him to be sure to come home before dark.

'Remember, now,' said his Dad, 'you'll
have to walk home through the woods!'
Promising he'd leave early, Sam set off
for Peter's house. He had a great time
reading stories and looking at the pictures
in some of Peter's exciting monster
books. Time flew by and when Sam
looked up he saw it was pitch dark.

'Oh no!' he gasped. 'I have to get home!'

Sam began to walk along the path through the dark woods. All of a sudden he heard a noise behind him.

He stopped. He heard a voice:

'Guess what I can do with my long bony finger and my ruby red lips?'

Sam yelped and started to run, but as he ran he heard pounding footsteps behind him.

Out of breath, he stopped and said: 'Who's there?'

But all he heard was the voice saying:

'Guess what I can do with my long bony finger and my ruby red lips?'

Sam ran on and on with the footsteps following behind him.

Once more he stopped and asked: 'Who's there?'

'Guess what I can do with my long bony finger and my ruby red lips?'

Poor Sam took to his heels again and raced on with the footsteps still behind him.

He stopped again and said: 'Look, who *is* it?'

'Guess what I can do with my long bony finger and my ruby red lips?'

Sam ran on down the path in front of his own house but when he reached the front door he found it was locked! He could still hear the footsteps behind him and again he called out: 'Who's there?'

'Guess what I can do with my long bony finger and my ruby red lips?'

Sam gulped and with his very last bit of courage he asked: 'Who are you and what

can you do with your long bony finger
and your ruby red lips?'

And the big creature behind him went:

✳ 'BmBmBmBmBmBmBmBmBm' ✳

*(Move finger up and down over loosely closed
and pursed lips, saying the letter B.)*

'Sam, did I not tell you to come home
before dark?'

'You did, Daddy,' said Sam.

'Well, Sam, I thought I'd sneak up on
you and give you a scare for a change!'

✳   ✳   ✳

Next time *you* want to scare one of your
friends you could try sneaking up behind
them and saying:

'Guess what I can do with my long bony
finger and my ruby red lips?'

And what *can* you do with your long
bony finger and your ruby red lips?

✳ 'BmBmBmBmBmBmBmBmBm' ✳

Rathlin Fairy Tale

A traditional story from County Antrim,
in which Jim meets the 'wee folk'.

Off the north-east coast of Ireland lies an island called Rathlin. It's a beautiful place with deep caves and rocky cliffs where many birds nest.

Long ago, a little boy called Jim lived on Rathlin Island with his mother, and every year Jim loved to go off to pick blackberries which his mother made into the most delicious jam. He always wore his oldest clothes – his tattered tweed trousers and his old baggy hand-knit jumper – because he usually came home covered in muck and dirt.

One afternoon before he set off his mother gave the usual warning: 'Now, you come home before it gets dark, and don't go near the fairy tree.'

All over Ireland you can see hawthorn trees standing in fields all by themselves. Some people call them fairy thorns and often farmers won't cut them down for fear of annoying the 'wee folk'. Jim's mother knew the old fairy stories and she was taking no chances!

While Jim was away his mother worked about the farm. Knowing how hungry Jim would be when he came back, she made his favourite meal of champ, which was mashed potatoes mixed with scallions heated in milk. It was all ready to eat and darkness was coming down – but there was no sign of Jim. His mother went outside, carrying her hurricane lamp, and called his name: 'Jim! Jim!' But her voice just echoed back on the wind.

She called her friends and neighbours and together they started a search which lasted the whole night through. They searched the rocky cliff paths and combed the beaches, but the little boy had vanished.

Jim's mother kept on hoping and praying, but by the next evening she had given up. She sat at the kitchen table with her head in her hands, weeping. Then, all of a sudden, she heard the door open and footsteps on the tiled floor. She looked up – and there before her was Jim! She blinked back the tears and stared, hardly believing her eyes. He was so different! His face was scrubbed and clean, his hair neatly parted, and his clothes – they looked as though they were brand new!

There were no holes in the trousers, no pulls on the jumper.

Jim's mother hugged him tightly.

'Where have you been, son?' she asked. 'What happened to you?'

And then Jim started to tell his story:

'I was coming home from picking black-berries and it was just getting dark when I saw this big bush full of berries at the foot of the fairy tree. I started to pick them and put them into my basket when all of a sudden I felt myself being nipped and pinched, and when I looked down I saw all these tiny wee people, no higher than my knees –'

'The fairies!' gasped his mother.

'Suddenly I felt myself being lifted up and up, and then I fell down, down the hollow trunk of the tree. When I hit the bottom I was lying inside the fairy rath and then I was plunged into a big bath

full of soapy water. Some of the wee people scrubbed my face and neck, others pulled at my old clothes. They took them away and washed them in another tub, and little tailors sat with their legs crossed, darning and stitching.'

Then Jim's mother remembered what the old people used to say. They said that if the fairies captured a human boy or girl they would try to clean them of all the dirt and grime of the world we live in. If they could remove every trace of our world in one day, they could keep that child forever in their world. People said this had happened a lot in the old days.

But Jim was home safe and sound. How could this be? How had he escaped? His mother didn't know how or why, but she was right glad of it. She put him to bed and they both thanked

God for his safe return.

At about ten o'clock that night his mother heard Jim shouting: 'Mammy, come quick!'

When she ran to his side he was sitting up in bed holding out his right hand. 'My finger's sore!'

Jim's mother took his small hand in

hers and when she looked at it closely she saw that deep down under the nail of his middle finger was a thorn from a blackberry bush. Those clever fairies, with all their cleaning and scrubbing, had somehow missed that little thorn. But it was just enough of a link with our world to bring Jim back home safe and sound.

The Rabbit's Tale

*A folk tale with a moral twist – and
absolutely true, of course!*

Rabbits these days have long ears and short fluffy tails, but did you know that the very first rabbit wasn't like that at all? He had tiny little ears like a hamster and a big, long, bushy tail like a fox. That first rabbit was a very proud creature who hopped through the forest making fun of any animal whose tail was smaller than his.

He'd often pick on the mouse saying: 'What a stupid-looking tail. That's just

like an old piece of string!' And the little
mouse would scurry away all upset.

Finally the mouse complained to the
fox, as he was the most cunning animal in
the wood. The fox decided to sort out
that tiresome rabbit once and for all.

'Just you leave him to me!' said the fox.

That very evening as the rabbit was hop-
ping home through the wood he saw the
fox sitting beside a pond.

'What are you doing sitting there?'
asked the rabbit.

'I'm fishing,' replied the fox, and when
the rabbit looked more closely he saw that
the fox's long tail was hanging down into
the water.

'What do you mean, fishing?'

'Well,' said the fox, 'it's a special trick. I
sit here very still and the fish get caught
up in my tail. Then I flick them out on to
the bank.'

'I don't care for fish myself,' said the rabbit, 'but I bet I can catch more than you with my fine bushy tail.' The boastful creature hopped over and sat down beside the fox. Very carefully he dropped his long tail – plop! – down into the pond.

The rabbit and the fox sat and sat and sat, but of course they didn't catch a single fish. It was getting dark and a cold wind began to blow through the trees.

'Brrrr!' said fox. 'It's too cold. I'm going home.'

'Cold? It's not a bit cold,' scoffed the rabbit. '*I'm* not giving up!'

As the fox moved off into the trees the rabbit sat by the pond, feeling prouder than ever of his magnificent tail. He would show them all how well he could fish! He sat and sat and sat. It began to get colder and colder. Then it got darker and darker and the rabbit began to shiver.

His long teeth started to chatter and he was shaking all over.

Finally he'd had enough. He decided to give up and hop off home. So he looked around to make sure no-one was watching, and then he tried to pull his tail out of the pond. But it wouldn't budge! It was stuck in a solid block of ice!

'Help! Help!' he shouted, but of course there was no-one around. He pulled and tugged but it was no good, he was stuck fast.

He crouched on his powerful back legs and prepared to jump, but he couldn't move an inch. He twisted and turned and stretched and strained, but the tail still wouldn't budge.

By morning he was almost frozen stiff. At last he noticed a large bird flying down over the pond.

The rabbit called out in a feeble voice: 'Help! Help!'

The bird flew over to him. 'What's wrong?' he said.

'C-could you p-please help me! My tail is stuck in the ice,' stuttered the rabbit.

'No trouble at all,' replied the bird.

He caught hold of the rabbit's two ears with his long talons. He started to pull. He pulled and he pulled – but the only thing that was happening was that the rabbit's ears were getting longer and longer!

He tried again. **P–u–l–l. S–t–r–e–t–c–h.**

At last there was a CRACK! The ice broke and the rabbit was free. He shot up out of the ice.

But when the bird put him down the rabbit turned round to examine his tail. To his horror he saw that his wonderful bushy tail had snapped off and most of it was still stuck in the ice! All he had left was a tiny little powder puff – *and* he had two long ears as well!

So that's the reason why today's rabbits have long ears and short tails. It's also why if you meet a rabbit in the park or in the fields he doesn't hop right up to you. You'll notice that he runs away instead and dives into the closest rabbit hole because he's so ashamed of his little fluffy tail!

Wee Meg Barnileg

*(Based on a story found in Ruth Sawyer's
The Way of the Storyteller)*

Wee Meg Barnileg was an only child. Now, her parents thought she was the most wonderful girl, but to tell you the truth she was spoilt rotten!

She wouldn't eat a thing her mother made for her. 'I don't like that! I can't eat that!' she'd say, and instead of telling her just to eat it up, her mother would coax her and plead with her, or would make two or three different things just for Meg.

When it came to clothes she was every

bit as bad. 'I can't wear *that!* I hate that!'
She'd change her clothes two or three
times a day.

Still, her parents thought she was the
best child ever, even if the neighbours
knew different! Her parents would say
she was a very 'observing' sort of girl –

what that really meant was that she was bold and outspoken. If she came to visit she would say things like: 'Oh look, Mammy, they've still got the same old curtains they had here last year!' or 'Look, Daddy, there's a big chip in this cup!' People dreaded her visits.

One of her worst faults was that she liked to tease animals. Now, one harvest time her parents took her to a farm and while they were inside talking Meg crept up on the old farm dog who was lying chained up in the yard. She leapt forward and yanked his tail, but quick as a flash he jumped up and nipped her on the leg.

'Waah!' Well, you could have heard her scream at the other end of the country!

Her parents came running, the farmer and his wife came running, the neighbours and friends came running. They all gathered around. Some people said the

dog should be put down – other people
muttered they'd be better getting rid of
that horrible child. When Meg heard this
she slipped away up to the hay field
where some men were working.

Now, they had left their lunches in
under the hedge to keep them cool.

What do you think Meg did? She sneaked in under the hedge and started helping herself to the bread and cheese and the bits of cake. Anything she didn't like she just tossed aside in the grass.

After a while she felt tired. She lay down and fell asleep. When she opened her eyes again she was amazed to see it was night time. There was a big harvest moon shining in the sky. All of a sudden she thought she heard whispering voices.

'Huh! Some dancing we're going to have tonight! That Meg girl has ruined our dancing floor with all these bits of food. If I could only get my hands on her I'd give her something to think about!'

Well, anyone else hearing people say that would have the wit to lie low, but not our Meg! Up she got as bold as brass with her hands on her hips!

'Well, here I am! What would you do?'

She blinked in amazement, for there in front of her was a ring of little people no taller than her knee – the fairy folk!

When they saw Meg they joined hands and started to circle round and round her, chanting a rhyme:

'Ring, ring, fairy ring, fairies dance and fairies sing. She'll move neither hand nor foot!'

And do you know, she couldn't! Meg wasn't able to move or talk, and before her eyes the fairies pulled up a big tuft of grass and disappeared under the ground, trailing Meg after them.

She found herself in a large underground chamber filled from floor to ceiling with rotten food – there were pieces of stale bread, lumps of cold porridge, slimy bits of cabbage.

'Do you see that?' said one of the wee men. 'That's all the good food you've wasted over the years. You'll get not a

bite to eat nor a sup to drink till you've got all of that swept up.'

Handing her a brush and shovel, he and the other wee men left her to it. What choice had she? Meg started to sweep the rubbish into piles and she shovelled it into a deep pit. By morning the work was done.

'Can I go home now?' she asked when they came to see how she had got on.

'No, you can't!' they roared. 'There's plenty more to do.' They gave her a slice of wheaten bread and a cup of buttermilk, and Meg was so glad to get it she thought it was the most wonderful food in the world.

They took her into a second room, filled from floor to ceiling with old clothes – torn clothes, dirty clothes.

'Do you see that?' asked one of the wee men. 'Those are all the clothes you have left lying behind you all those years for your poor mother to clean and mend. You'll not get another bite to eat nor a sup to drink until you've got all those washed, mended and ironed.'

What choice had she? Meg started to work, and she worked on and on until she could hardly straighten her back. At last there were piles of clean, neatly pressed clothes beside her. 'Can I go home now?' she begged.

'No, you can't! There's still more work to be done.'

After giving her some more bread and milk they brought her into a third room which was full of tall spiky weeds. Here and there between the weeds Meg could see a pretty pink flower, or a yellow flower, or a blue flower.

'Oh that's terrible,' she said. 'The pretty flowers will be choked by all those old weeds.'

'Hmm! Glad you noticed,' said one of the wee folk. 'Those weeds are all the nasty, horrible things you've said over the years, and those pretty flowers are the few pleasant things you've ever had to say about anything. Don't you think it's time you set things right?'

This time Meg didn't need any coaxing. She started to weed, and she worked until her hands were all blistered. And when she finished the weeds had all gone.

'There now,' she said at last, 'don't the flowers look better? I'm sorry for saying all those nasty things.'

The next thing she knew, Meg found herself up above the ground. The harvest moon was shining and the fairies were dancing around in a ring.

Now, you'll remember that Meg was a very 'observing' sort of girl? Well, she knew that if a human boy or girl was

taken away by the fairies the only sure
way to get home again was to find a four-
leafed clover and make a wish. As she
danced around with the fairies she kept
her eyes peeled and sure enough she
spotted a four-leafed clover. Quick as a
flash she grabbed it and said: 'I wish I
was back in my own bed!'

And the very next minute she was! She
opened her eyes – and there was her
mother leaning over her.

'Oh, Mammy, I'm sorry I teased that dog. He wouldn't have bitten me if I hadn't!'

'Glory be!' said her mother. 'Our Meg's back to us again.'

It turned out that Meg had been lying there in her bed not able to speak or move for a year and a day. She had been away with the fairies all that time.

From that day on Meg was a changed girl. She ate whatever was put in front of her, she wore the clothes her mother left out for her, and until the day she died she always had a good word for everybody.

A Riddle Story

Two Legs sat on Three Legs
eating No Legs.

In came Four Legs, snatched up No Legs
and ran off.

Then Two Legs grabbed Three Legs
and threw it after Four Legs –

And Four Legs then dropped No Legs
on the floor!

Can you guess what this riddle is about?
Try to see the pictures in your head! Here goes:

Two Legs is a person

Three Legs is a stool

No Legs is a fish

And Four Legs is a cat

So this is what the riddle means:

A person sat on a stool eating a fish.

In came a cat, snatched up the fish
and ran off.

The person grabbed the stool
and threw it after the cat –

And the cat dropped the fish on the floor!

So, here's the riddle again:

Two Legs sat on Three Legs eating No Legs.

In came Four Legs, snatched up No Legs
and ran off.

Then Two Legs grabbed Three Legs
and threw it after Four Legs –

And Four Legs then dropped No Legs
on the floor!

The Tailor and the Button

A traditional tale, with repetition,
in which everyone can take part.

Once there was a tailor who was
the best in all the land. He made
a suit of clothes for the king and the
king was so pleased with his fine new
outfit that he decided to give the tailor
a special gift.

Now, he wondered what the tailor
would like. He had a horse, and he
seemed to be making plenty of money.
Yet the tailor was always dressed in rags.

The king decided that the tailor needed
new clothes, for he never got around to
making clothes for himself. So the king
gave the tailor the finest piece of cloth
that money could buy.

When the
tailor saw
the cloth he
decided there
was enough in it
to make himself
a new COAT.
So he cut out the coat
and he stitched it up and he put it on.
It was the finest coat he had ever had in
his life. And he wore that coat . . .
and he wore that coat . . . and he wore that
coat until it was all worn out – at least, he
thought it was worn out, but when he
looked again he saw there was just enough
good material left to make himself a JACKET.

So he cut out the jacket and he stitched
it up and he put it on. It was the finest
jacket he had ever had in his life. And
he wore that jacket . . . and he wore
that jacket . . . and he wore that
jacket until it was all worn out,
at least he thought it was worn
out, but when he looked
again he saw there was
just enough
material left
to make a
WAISTCOAT.

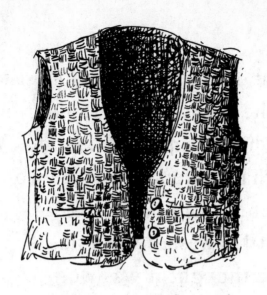

So he cut out the waistcoat and he
stitched it up and he put it on. It was the
finest waistcoat he had ever had in his life.
And he wore that waistcoat . . . and he
wore that waistcoat . . . and he wore that
waistcoat until it was all worn out – at
least he *thought* it was worn out, but when
he looked again he saw there was just
enough material left to make a CAP.

So he cut out the cap and he stitched it up and he put it on. It was the finest cap he had ever had in his life. And he wore that cap . . . and he wore that cap . . . and he wore that cap until it was all worn out – at least he *thought* it was worn out, but when he looked again he saw there was just enough material left to make a **TIE**.

So he cut out the tie and he stitched it up and he put it on. It was the finest tie he had ever had in his life.

And he wore that tie . . . and he wore that
tie . . . and he wore that tie until it was all
worn out – at least he *thought* it was
worn out, but when he looked again he
saw there was just enough material left
to make a **BUTTON**.

So he cut out the button and he stitched
it up and he put it on. It was the finest
button he had ever had in his life.

Every time he looked at that button it
reminded him of so many things. It
reminded him of the king and the suit
of clothes he had made for the king.

It reminded him of the cloth and the COAT and the JACKET and the WAIST-COAT and the CAP and the TIE.

He wore that button . . . and he wore that button . . . and he wore that button until it was all worn out – at least he *thought* it was worn out, but when he looked at it again he saw there was just enough material left to make – a STORY.

Other books from
THE O'BRIEN PRESS
FOR YOUNGER CHILDREN

FULL-COLOUR PICTURE BOOKS

LITTLE STAR
MARITA CONLON-MCKENNA
Illustrated by Christopher Coady
A bright star falls to earth and becomes James's playmate.
Paperback £4.50

MR BEAR BABYSITS
Written and illustrated by DEBI GLIORI
Mr Bear finds out the hard way how to handle the little grizzlies!
Paperback £4.50

MR BEAR'S PICNIC
Written and illustrated by DEBI GLIORI
An idyllic picnic day, but the little grizzlies give Mr Bear lots of trouble!
Paperback £4.50

FRED
LINDA JENNINGS
Illustrated by Basia Bogdanowicz
Fred is terrified of his little cat door, until he finally learns to be brave!
Paperback £4.50

GUESS HOW MUCH I LOVE YOU
SAM McBRATNEY
Illustrated by Anita Jeram
Who loves whom the most? Little Nut-brown Hare, or Big Hare?
Hardback £7.99

IRISH LEGENDS

THE BOYNE VALLEY BOOK AND TAPE
BRENDA MAGUIRE

Illustrated by Peter Haigh

Recorded by Gay Byrne, Cyril Cusack, Maureen Potter, John B. Keane, Rosaleen Linehan, Twink.

Over an hour of storytelling from the great Irish tradition.

Paperback book and tape £6.95

LITTLE PIGGIES
PAUL MORGAN & SALLY MORGAN

This little piggy went to ... a party. And what a party it is!!

Paperback £4.25

NOAH'S ARK
JANE RAY

Every child's favourite Bible story, with exquisite illustrations.

Paperback £4.99

OWL BABIES
MARTIN WADDELL

Illustrated by Patrick Benson

Mother has gone to hunt and the little owls anxiously await her return.

Paperback £4.50

SAILOR BEAR
MARTIN WADDELL

Illustrated by Virginia Austin

Going to sea looks very exciting – until Little Sailor Bear *does* it!

Paperback £4.50

THE PIG IN THE POND
MARTIN WADDELL

Illustrated by Jill Barton

There's more than a *pig* in the pond – Farmer Neligan ends up there too!

Paperback £4.50

THE HAPPY PRINCE

OSCAR WILDE

Illustrated by Jane Ray

Wilde's famous story stunningly illustrated, with special gold printing.

Paperback £5.50

And many more, for adults and children.
Send for our full-colour catalogue.

ORDER FORM

These books are available from your local bookseller. In case of difficulty
order direct from THE O'BRIEN PRESS

Please send me the books as marked
I enclose cheque / postal order for £......... (+ 50p P&P per title)
OR please charge my credit card ☐ Access / Mastercard ☐ Visa

Card number ☐☐☐☐ ☐☐☐☐ ☐☐☐☐ ☐☐☐☐

EXPIRY DATE ☐ ☐ ☐ ☐

Name: ....Tel: ....

Address: ....

....

THE O'BRIEN PRESS
20 Victoria Road, Dublin 6, Ireland
Tel: (01) 4923333 Fax: (01) 4922777